The SUMMER I Lost It

by Natalie Kath

STONE ARCH BOOKS
a capstone imprint

The Summer I Lost It is published by Stone Arch Books
A Capstone Imprint
1710 Roe Crest Drive,
North Mankato, Minnesota 56003
www.capstonepub.com

Library of Congress Cataloging-in-Publication Data is available on the Library of Congress website.

ISBN: 978-1-4342-3316-5 (library binding)
ISBN: 978-1-4342-4067-5 (softcover)

Summary: Kat is just like other fourteen-year-old girls. Except that this summer, she's taking charge of her life and finally losing weight. But can she do it?

Photo Credits: Shutterstock: Erhan Dayi, YanLev

Designer: Emily Harris
Art Director: Kay Fraser
Production Specialist: Michelle Biedscheid

Printed in the United States of America in Brainerd, Minnesota.
102011   006406BANGS12

The SUMMER I Lost It

by Natalie Kath

I'm Kat, and I'm fat.

I'm not just overweight or curvy or pleasantly plump.
I don't just have baby fat. My doctor told me that
I need to lose fifteen pounds just to get out of the
"obese" category.

We're supposed to write a journal this summer
for school. They're not going to read it, but they'll
make sure it's written in. We have to write every day
for seven entire weeks. About, like, our hopes and
dreams, I guess. Well, I HOPE that I can convince
my mom and dad to let me go to fat camp this
summer. I DREAM about not being fat anymore. I
WISH I could snap my fingers and be thin.

All of my friends are excited about summer. Not me.

I don't want to wear a T-shirt and jeans at the beach. I don't want to tell my friends that I don't want to swim, when really I just don't want to wear a swimsuit in front of everyone. I don't want to hang out at the mall, looking at clothes that would never fit me, seeing myself in mirrors next to my pretty, thin friends. I don't want to go to movies where the fat girl is always the funny sidekick. I don't want to be the funny, fat sidekick. I want to have a boyfriend. I want to feel better about myself. I want to be healthier.

This summer, I want to change. This summer is going to be different.

♡

Kat

JUNE

SUNDAY	MONDAY
10	**11**

* Start journaling for summer project

THURSDAY	FRIDAY
14	**15**

TUESDAY	WEDNESDAY
12 William's baseball game	**13**
SATURDAY	
16 Emily's party!	

Sunday, June 10

I've been trying to think about hopes and dreams.
All I can think about is losing weight. When Aunt
Wendy was 35, she went to fat camp. She tells
everyone how amazing it was. That it totally changed
her life. She's not super skinny now, but she's healthy
and active and she always eats well. She told me that
she wishes she'd gone when she was my age.

And that got me thinking. What if I went to fat
camp this summer? I totally could. I looked it up,
and there's even one here in Wisconsin. So I talked
to Mom and Dad today. After dinner, I gave them all
of the research I'd done on fat camps for kids my age.
Then I begged.

They said they'd talk about it tonight and let me know tomorrow. Now I'm too excited and nervous to sleep. This could totally change my life.

What if I get to go?

What if I start freshman year as the hottest girl in school?

What if I finally get a boyfriend?

What if tomorrow is the first day of my fabulous new life?

I don't want next year to start the same way every other year has. I want to change. I know I can do it.

Kat

They said no.

They said it costs thousands of dollars. We just can't afford it. Whatever.

Deep down I knew that's what they'd say, but that doesn't make me any less mad about it. I really wanted this to be the summer I got healthy. Instead, it's just going to be the same as every other summer.

I start it fat, and I end it fat.

I spent all day in my room, watching movies and eating chips. If my parents don't care about me losing weight, why should I?

I might as well get used to being fat, because I will be for the rest of my life. And I might as well get used to the fact that this is going to be the worst summer of all time.

Kat

I woke up today feeling horrible. I'm still mad at my parents, and more than that, I just feel really depressed. I feel like I'm stuck in this body, this unhealthy body. It's not me.

The day didn't get any better, either. I sat around and watched TV all day, until it was time to go to William's baseball game. I was not in the mood, but Mom made me go. She said I had to because in our family we support each other. I had to laugh. Where was my support when I asked to go to fat camp, and they shot me down?

The day improved for a minute when Josh came and sat by me at the game.

I forgot that his brother is on William's team.

Josh is so adorable, with his dimples and curly brown hair! But I know he only thinks of me as a friend. The fat girl is always "just a friend."

We went to get a soda between innings, and we ran into his grandma at the concession stand. When Josh introduced me, she said, "Oh, dear, you have the prettiest face!" I was mortified! I know what she really meant. She meant, "You have a pretty face — too bad the rest of you is so fat."

I wanted to die.

Kat

I couldn't sleep last night. I kept thinking about what that old lady had said. I guess that's what happens when you're called Fat Kat for fourteen years.

I got up and checked Facebook, and then it hit me. You can find anything online.

So I started digging, and found a ton of information on exercise plans, eating right, strength movements, and running training schedules. I bookmarked a few beginner pages.

Something clicked. I don't need a million-dollar fat camp to get healthy. I can do it on my own. Maybe my parents don't care enough, but I do.

TO DO LIST

1. Call Aunt Wendy for tips
2. Buy cute workout clothes
3. Buy good shoes
4. Gym??? Ask Mom and Dad for loan to cover costs?
5. Make healthy food plans
6. Grocery store

Thursday, June 14

Before I had a chance to talk to Mom and Dad about my new plan, they came to talk to me. They said they would get me a gym membership, if I was interested. Which I was, of course.

Then they sweetened the deal. (You could tell they felt really bad about the fat camp thing.)

If I can lose 15 pounds in the next five weeks, starting Sunday, they'll take me to WildWater Park for vacation. We went there a couple of years ago, and I loved it. And if I lose 15 pounds, I won't feel as nervous about being in a swimsuit.

Okay, I totally need to lose more than fifteen pounds. But I guess they've been doing some research of their own, and Mom said it wasn't healthy to lose weight faster than that (even if on TV people sometimes lose that in one week).

So tomorrow I'm going to go to Aunt Wendy's gym. I'm really nervous. I've never even been inside a real gym. I've only seen them on TV, so I picture them full of over-tanned, skinny girls with perfect makeup. I hope it's not really like that, or I won't feel comfortable there AT ALL.

I'm scared.

Kat

Friday, June 15

I am officially a gym member. The place is enormous. When I signed up, I got a tour, so now I don't feel as overwhelmed. There are about three hundred treadmills, exercise bikes, elliptical machines, weights, you name it. They even have yoga classes and a swimming pool. I don't know if I'll be brave enough to try most of it. Maybe.

So I'm starting tomorrow. They give you three free sessions with a personal trainer when you join the gym. I'm going to see Aunt Wendy's trainer, Stephanie. She seemed cool when we met.

I also got my mom and dad to help me make an appointment with a nutritionist.

I'm actually not worried about working out. I like sports and being active. Changing how I eat is going to be the hardest part.

I love food. I love salty food. I love sweets. I love butter. I love bread almost as much as I love life itself. I am NOT going to give up my faves. I hope I can figure out a way to eat what I love and lose weight. It's got to be possible, right?

In other news, Emily is having a party this weekend. And she told me she's inviting Josh. I wish it were possible to lose weight by Saturday!

Kat

Tomorrow is the official start of my challenge. So I had to weigh myself today.

Let's just say that I had no idea what I was in for. I hadn't weighed myself in months. I get weighed at the doctor's office when I go in for a physical, but I never look at the number. So I had no idea what to expect.

I used the scale in Mom and Dad's bathroom. I read online that you should weigh yourself at the same time of day each time, so I decided to do it before my shower.

I made sure the door was locked. Then I took off my clothes and stepped carefully onto the scale.

Then I jumped right back off.

Then I cried.

Luckily, that was pretty early this morning, so my face had de-puffed by the time I met Stephanie at the gym for my first training session. She took me around to what felt like every machine in the building. My arms were so tired by the time I got done, I could barely take my ponytail out. Steph said I'd be really sore in a couple of days.

I ran a mile on the treadmill. Well, okay, I walked most of it. It was exhausting and felt like it took forever. I'm going back tomorrow. If I can move.

Kat

JUNE

SUNDAY	MONDAY
17	**18** Lunch w/Emily and Mackenzie at McDonalds

THURSDAY	FRIDAY
21 *Session w/Stephanie *Movie/dinner w/Em and Mac	**22** Jog!

TUESDAY	WEDNESDAY
19 Nutritionist, 11 a.m.	**20** Jog!

SATURDAY	
23 Weigh-in Day	

Sunday, June 17

Last night was Emily's party. I almost didn't go. I'm trying to eat healthier, and I knew there would be a ton of stuff I shouldn't eat.

I wish I could like live in a protective bubble that only has healthy food and opportunity for exercise. A place where I could go to work on myself, while the rest of the world stands still.

On the other hand, I knew Josh was going, so I had to go. I did show up a little late, and I made myself eat a healthy dinner beforehand so I wouldn't have room for chips and dip and ice cream.

As soon as I got there, I felt like it was a mistake.

Josh was there, but so was Alexis. I asked Emily why she invited Alexis, but Em said she didn't — that Josh had just brought her along. Obviously that made me feel awful. She's everything I'm not.

I feel so stupid for thinking that maybe Emily's party could be the perfect opportunity for Josh to really notice me. What was I thinking? His grandma basically pointed out how fat I am. Alexis is tiny and bubbly and adorable. Why would Josh be interested in me when she's around?

Kat

Monday, June 18

Stephanie wasn't kidding around! I thought she was full of it when she said I'd be sorest a few days after my first time at the gym. Yesterday I was okay. I didn't work out, I just went for a walk outside, but I could move. My arms were a little sore, but nothing too bad.

This morning it hit. Getting out of bed was awful. Every single inch of me hurt. It makes sense, I guess. I've had to run before in gym, but I never lifted weights. I hurt in places I didn't even know I had muscles! I wanted to just go back to bed, but I had the urge to keep my muscles moving. Somehow, I just knew it would make me feel better.

So I went for a walk with my dog, Betty. By the time I got back, my legs were feeling pretty good. I figured the worst was over, but when I tried to wash my hair in the shower, I could barely raise my arms!

This is ridiculous! How do they expect people to get in shape when you can't move for days at a time? It hurts too much to even write!

Kat

I could finally move this morning. I forgot what it felt like to be nearly pain-free. I had Dad measure out a mile route for me, so I went for a run this morning. I walked a couple of blocks, but ran the rest of the way.

I felt so good when I was done! Then I went to my nutritionist appointment. Man, that was a wake-up call. Lisa, the nutritionist, asked me what I'd been eating for the past few days.

I thought it was pretty healthy — I ate a salad at McDonald's yesterday instead of a burger, and I've been trying to have fruit instead of chips.

I was shocked when Lisa showed me the nutrition information for the fast-food salad.

She said it's always better to choose fresh fruits and vegetables, but I have to be careful about the calories in the salad dressing. She basically said fast food isn't a good idea at all — even if it's a salad. And she told me that I should cut out salt, because that makes you extra puffy. I don't need any more puffiness.

To lose weight, I'm going to need to eat around 1800 calories a day. Lisa said it's really important to make sure I'm eating enough, especially since I'm going to be exercising a lot. She also said I should do one free day a week, where I can eat whatever I want. I've never counted calories before. It's kind of a pain, but I'll get used to it. I guess I can try.

Kat

McD's salad: 430 calories

Big Mac: 540 calories

1 apple: 80 calories

small bag of chips: 250 calories

Wednesday, June 20

Yesterday, Lisa told me to make a list of my goals. She said it's really helpful to have that to look at while I work on cutting calories and being healthier in general. I guess it's supposed to motivate me or something. I don't know, I think it could help, I guess, but I'm not sure how writing it down makes a difference.

But I told Lisa I would, so I will.

Kat

GOALS

- Lose 15 pounds
- Run 3x/week (at least one mile)
- Lift weights 1x/week
- Ride bike (as cardio) 1x/week (at least 5 miles)
- Keep calories between 1500–1800 per day except for Sunday
- Eat vegetables when I need a snack
- Sunday: a day of rest, and I can have one "free" meal (whatever I want)
- Look better in a swimsuit
- Feel better about myself
- Treat myself better
- Get a boyfriend

Thursday, June 21

Stephanie's parents should have named her Sarge.
She makes me feel like I'm at boot camp during our
sessions! I had my second free session today. We did
even more of the machines. I didn't cry. Small victory
for me. When we were done, her next client was
waiting. Steph said, "Oh, I think you guys are about
the same age! I should introduce you." His name is
Connor. He is adorable! Dark curly hair and dimples!
SO CUTE! Of course I blushed and stuttered and
generally acted like an idiot. Oh well. I'm not at the
gym to meet guys.

Tonight I tried to go out with Mackenzie and Emily.
It was brutal. I still haven't told them about trying to
lose weight. I'm not sure why. I guess it's just kind of
embarrassing.

We went to a movie, which was fine. I said my stomach was bothering me, so I didn't have any candy. Then everyone wanted to go grab a snack at Jenny's Grill. Nothing but fried food as far as the eye could see. When I ordered a grilled chicken salad, instead of my usual hamburger, fries, and a shake, I finally had to 'fess up about my new lifestyle. Mac had a ton of questions. She wants to be my jogging partner. Emily didn't say much – she was too busy dipping her fries in mayo. Must be nice to not have to worry about what you eat.

Kat

grilled chicken salad:
420 calories

burger and shake meal deal:
1150 calories

Friday, June 22

Today my body totally rebelled. I am so tired. My
legs feel like they're made of concrete. Even smiling
seems like a lot of work. I tried to read a book today,
and I couldn't focus on the words.

I was way less sore this morning than last time after
Sarge's workout, but my body was exhausted. I had to
give myself a super pep-talk to get my jog in today.
After my shower, I completely crashed. I took a four-
hour nap!

How does anyone exercise and go to school? Or
work? Or have a life?

The thought of trying to sit through classes right now is unbearable. I thought they said you were supposed to have more energy when you exercise. I swear I read something about endorphins elevating your mood. No way.

Maybe my body is just broken or something.

I have never been more exhausted.

Kat

Saturday, June 23

I lay awake in bed for a while before I got up this morning. From the second I woke up, I knew I had to get on the scale. I was freaked out.

What if I didn't lose any weight? What if it was all for nothing? What if I gained weight?

I was so tired, I was ready to quit altogether. Maybe it wasn't worth it. Maybe I could learn to just like being fat. Maybe I'd just get used to it, and I'd be happy, and I wouldn't have to exercise or watch what I ate. I could just get fatter and fatter.

I pictured myself blowing up, like the girl in the Willy Wonka movie.

That made me laugh, which made me start feeling better. And feeling better reminded me that I didn't want to be fat BECAUSE I want to feel better!

And then I got up. I went to the scale. I took a deep breath, stepped on, and exhaled.

I finally looked down.

I lost 7 pounds!

There may have been some dancing done to celebrate.

Kat

JUNE

SUNDAY	MONDAY
24	**25**
Free day!!!	Run a mile

THURSDAY	FRIDAY
28	**29**
*Party at Meghan's ★ *Jog	Gym

TUESDAY	WEDNESDAY
26 Yoga 3 p.m.	**27** Weights???
SATURDAY	
30 Weigh-In	

When I told my mom I'd lost seven pounds, she got really worried. She made me list every food I'd eaten over the last week. I guess she thought it was too much weight to lose in a week. She even called my nutritionist to make sure she shouldn't freak out.

Lisa told her that cutting out salt and starting an exercise routine can make a person drop a lot of weight right away, but that it wouldn't keep going at that rate. Which, I'll admit, was a little depressing. Not that I want to lose seven pounds a week. But it would be nice to get it over with.

Today was my free day, so I got to pretend to be old Kat. Which of my faves did I want the most? Buffalo chicken sandwich and fries from Kelly's? Pizza from Eddie's downtown? The Italian sub from Cerini's?

I decided on pizza, and Mac came along. She spent most of the time talking about Luke. Recapping their conversation at Emily's party. Telling me, in detail, about how they flirt at Scoop Shop (like serving ice cream is so romantic). I tried to pay attention, but it was hard. I want a guy to flirt with. I want to have someone to talk to my friends about. I want someone to want to talk about me to their friends. I want someone to think I'm pretty, not just a fat girl with a pretty face.

Kat

Monday, June 25

I got up this morning ready to run! I guess yesterday's day off was all I needed to get motivated. Betty started jumping around when I put on my running shoes. She loves running with me.

We were almost done with our mile when I made a decision. I was going to go for two. I was tired, but not so tired that I couldn't keep going. So we headed out on our second loop. I had to walk for a while to get my breathing under control, but when I finally finished I was pretty happy. I pushed myself a little bit, and I did it!

Okay. Remember how I said I thought my body was broken? That I never felt good from exercise? Well, now I know what people mean when they say they got a runner's high. I felt amazing.

And I didn't even feel like I was going to fall down after I was done.

Aunt Wendy called today and said Sarge would let me crash one of their sessions every week for free! I guess of all the people in my family, Wendy understands the best what I'm trying to do. She dealt with being overweight for years, until she finally got it under control. I'd be lost without her.

Kat

This morning at breakfast (an egg-white omelet with chopped vegetables, a lowfat yogurt, and an orange) Mom told me that I'd inspired her to join the gym, too. A couple of women that she works with go to some of the classes after work, so she's going to as well. She said seeing me so full of energy made her want to feel better too.

What if I end up working out with my mom? Can you imagine the horror? I can see it now. She'd want to do all of our classes together. She'd reach over and wipe off my forehead if I got sweaty. She'd want to sit next to me on the spin bikes.

She'd match me step for step in Zumba. She'd rub my back during the meditation time in yoga. She'd totally want to come to my training sessions with Wendy and Sarge. And worst of all, if Connor was there and he so much as smiled at me, she would assume he was my boyfriend and invite him to dinner. Speaking of Connor, I haven't seen him since Steph introduced us. I keep hoping I'll bump into him at the gym, but no luck.

OMG. Do I have a crush on Connor?

I have been thinking about him a lot . . .

Kat

my breakfast: 342 calories
two fried eggs, hashbrowns,
bacon, and orange juice:
806 calories

I tried to take on the gym by myself today. I threw on my headphones, and headed to the weight area. I was busy keeping my head down, hoping no one noticed me, so I didn't see Connor. I was trying to move the pad on the hamstring machine when he tapped me on the shoulder. I jumped about a foot!

He asked if I'd like some help with the machine. I tried to act like I knew what I was doing, but I clearly didn't.

After he moved the pad, we chatted for a minute. He goes to Medford High, and he's going to be a sophomore.

He's been working with Sarge for about two months, and he laughed and laughed when I told him how I call her Sarge. He is so nice, and funny and cute!

Not even changing in the locker room had me in a panic today. I was off in my own little world. I was mentally writing our names with hearts around them. Kat and Connor. It has a nice ring to it.

Kat

Thursday, June 28

I opened my eyes this morning and smiled. What is it about a cute guy that makes everything just a little more tolerable? My run today flew by. I keep picturing Connor. I know it's silly. I barely know him. But I still smile every time I think about him.

My day didn't stay great, though, even though I tried really hard to stay in a good mood.

I went to Meghan's party tonight with Mac and Em, where reality slapped me in the face. Repeatedly.

Josh was there. I talked to him for a second, but the minute he walked away, he was talking to Alexis.

I get it. She's cute and fun, and skinny.

I ate way more than I should have, which didn't help. When I'm sad, I eat. It's not really a good excuse, but sometimes I can't help it.

I wish I could just stop liking Josh. I wish I was skinny. I wish I didn't have to work so hard. I wish Josh liked me. I wish I didn't always feel like the fat girl. I wish I didn't feel so alone.

Kat

I felt down all day today. I've had a crush on Josh for two years, and I'm finally realizing that he's never going to like me. Ever. He sees me as a friend, and that's it.

I was thinking about it while I ran on the treadmill at the gym, and I know it's true. Josh isn't ever going to see me as anything other than a friend.

There. Just writing it down makes it seem more true.

I'm not going to lie, it hurts.

I guess part of me thought if I just lost some weight, he'd like me. But Josh can't be the reason I'm doing this. I need to do it for myself.

Kat

Saturday, June 30

My weigh-in was today. I gained a pound.

I don't get it. How is it possible to work as hard as I have been and GAIN weight?

I'm so mad, and I can't stop crying.

I was so stupid to think I could do this on my own. I'll always be the fat girl. Always!

As soon as I got off the scale, I went into the kitchen. I wanted to make being fat worth it!

I was going to eat every fatty, sugary, salty thing I could find.

I rummaged through the cupboards for a minute until I remembered that Mom and I got rid of all the junk food when I started this new healthy lifestyle.

I've been in my room for the past four hours. I didn't work out. I skipped the gym. Not even the possibility of seeing Connor is going to bring me out of this. What's the point? I'm fat. He doesn't like me, and he won't. Ever.

Kat

JULY

SUNDAY	MONDAY
1 *Ice cream with Mac ---->BEACH!!!	**2**

THURSDAY	FRIDAY
5 Movie w/Mac and Em	**6** Sarge 10 a.m.

TUESDAY	WEDNESDAY
3	**4**
	Party at our house! *Fireworks*

SATURDAY	
7	
Weigh-in *Mac & Em coming for dinner*	

Sunday, July 1

I feel so stupid for how I acted yesterday. Like it was the end of the world that I gained a pound. I didn't even think about the fact that I'm still down six pounds. Six pounds in two weeks is pretty great.

Also, I didn't exactly eat right on Thursday night. I probably ate more salt that night than the rest of the week combined. Salt makes your body hang on to water, so that explains at least a little bit of the weight gain. Anyway, I'm over it now. Moving on.

I'm over something else, too.

Josh.

I saw him at William's baseball game. Today he was with Alexis, and when he saw me, he smiled and waved. His arm was around her.

Then it hit me. The fact that Josh is with Alexis doesn't say anything about me. All it says is that Josh likes Alexis.

So. Done with that drama. Back to making this the best summer ever! I'm going for a swim with Mac. And then, since it's Sunday, we're going to get ice cream. (But only one scoop.)

Kat

Scoop Shop Faves
lemon buttermilk (me)
pistachio (Mac)
chocolate chip (Em)

Monday, July 2

I was actually looking forward to my run today. But when I walked outside, it was about a million degrees out. Running at the gym sounded a lot better than running through the heat.

I walked in at the same time as Connor. He was going to his appointment with Sarge, so he didn't have time to talk, but he asked me if I was coming back tomorrow.

I hadn't planned on it, but when he said we should meet up to lift weights together, of course I said that was a great idea.

I'm sure I sounded like a stuttering fool. He said he'd meet me at the front desk at 10. I couldn't believe it. I was so excited! I'm sure I looked like a moron for my entire workout, smiling the whole time.

Then the panic hit. Cute guy. Heavy equipment. Me. I hope he doesn't think I'm a complete klutz.

Mac called me tonight, and kept going on and on and on about Luke and how much she likes him and how great he is. And for the first time in a long time, I didn't even bring up Josh. I just kept thinking about Connor and kind of smiling to myself. I can't wait until tomorrow.

Kat

Tuesday, July 3

I was so nervous this morning I thought I was going to barf. Seriously. For starters, I didn't know how to get ready. I don't have cute gym clothes – I have baggy t-shirts and shorts. I couldn't curl my hair or put on any makeup, since I knew I was going to be a sweaty mess.

And then there was the big question. I didn't know if it was a date, or just working out together, or what. Was it a friend thing, or a potential romantic thing? I almost called the gym to ask them to tell him that I couldn't make it. But at the last minute, I forced myself to go.

He was waiting when I got there, and we went up to the weight room. I didn't know how to work some of the machines, but he helped me out, and he never made me feel stupid about it.

We talked the whole time! I am usually pretty shy when it comes to talking to cute guys, but with him I wasn't. It was weird. We never ran out of things to talk about. The time went really fast.

Then, as we were leaving, he asked me if I wanted to go to a baseball game with him sometime!

That's a date, right?

Of course I said yes.

Kat

Wednesday, July 4

The Fourth of July. For my family, that means a huge cookout. We invite a ton of people, and everyone brings food. Usually there's at least three kinds of meat, bag after bag of chips, ten kinds of dip, four million plates of brownies or cake or cookies or whatever, and of course, ice cream.

Not this year. Well, all of that stuff was here this year, but I didn't eat it.

Mom and I found a recipe for turkey burgers online. She made those for me, and a couple of other people tried them too. They were really good.

Aunt Wendy brought this crazy chocolate tofu mousse thing. I thought it was going to taste weird, but it was actually great.

And then I had watermelon for dessert.

It's funny. Usually I spend the evening of the Fourth lying around, waiting for fireworks, and feeling really tired, even though I haven't done anything. Not this year. I played volleyball for like three hours, and I was wide awake at fireworks time. It was a fun day. Even without the junk food.

Kat

One cup of watermelon: 46 calories

One cup of vanilla ice cream: 289 calories

Thursday, July 5

Tonight, I met up with Mac and Em for a movie.
Afterward, they wanted to go get something to eat.
We went to Kelly's. They ordered up their usual fried
deliciousness. I was tempted to order something like
that, but then I remembered what happened last
week. Salad for me, thank you.

While we waited for the food to come, Mac kept
saying, "You look different!" She'd nudge Em and
say, "Doesn't she look different?" Em seemed kind of
uncomfortable about it. But Mac just kept going on
and on about how I looked happier, glowy, whatever.

I didn't tell them about Connor. I don't know why.

For some reason, I wanted to keep that as all mine.
I didn't feel like sharing. I didn't want to answer any
questions, or describe him, or anything like that.
Maybe part of me was afraid that I'd jinx it if I talked
about it, I don't know.

Anyway, I just kind of smiled and said I felt great,
and then we started talking about other stuff. Like
how I'm finally over Josh. Emily looked really
relieved when I said that. It turns out that she knew
that Josh and Alexis liked each other, and she felt
really bad about it since she knew I liked Josh. I'm so
glad I'm not hung up on him anymore!

Kat

Friday, July 6

Sarge had me run a mile today while she timed me. Gross. That took me right back to gym class. But I did it.

I started to run, and my brain took off, too. I started thinking about Josh. The truth is, I've never had a real reason for liking him. Nothing ever happened that made me think he was worth worshipping for two years. Yeah, his locker was next to mine in seventh grade. And yeah, he was cute. But there are plenty of other cute guys at my school.

The only difference is that he talked to me. I mean, a lot of people talk to me. But Josh talked to me like a real person.

I always thought he could see past my weight and into my real self.

The mile was over before I knew it. Sarge was smiling when I was done. She said I'd done pretty well. Twelve minutes. Not marathon material, but way better than I did last year in gym class.

Maybe letting go of Josh is helping me run faster.

Kat

Saturday, July 7

I was so nervous this morning about weighing myself. Yeah, I'd eaten better this week, and I'd definitely been hitting the gym as much as I could.

But what if I still gained? This week was make it or break it. If I gained weight this week, there was no way I'd lose fifteen pounds in time to meet my parents' challenge. Say goodbye to a fun vacation, and say goodbye to the best summer ever. I might as well give up.

But I had to weigh myself.

Thank goodness, I was down three pounds from last week. That's a total of nine. NINE.

I'm totally on track!

The good stuff just kept coming. This afternoon, Connor texted me to see if I wanted to go to the baseball game on Monday afternoon! I had to hold myself back so I didn't respond in two seconds. I waited a couple of minutes. Then I told him I'd love to. He's going to get back to me tomorrow with the plan. I am so excited! My stomach has been doing flips since I got his text!

Em and Mac came over for dinner (taco salads), and I told them all about Connor. They're both coming over tomorrow to help figure out what I'm going to wear.

Kat

SUNDAY	MONDAY
8 Session w/ Sarge and Aunt Wendy, 10 a.m.	**9** Baseball game with Connor

THURSDAY **12**	FRIDAY **13**
Run	Weights?

TUESDAY	WEDNESDAY
10 Gym	**11** Free day!!!

SATURDAY **14**	
weigh-in hang out at Mac's	

Sunday, July 8

I had my first session with Sarge and Aunt Wendy this morning. That was really good news. If I'd sat around at home all day, I would've gone insane!

Today, we focused on legs – lunges and squats and step ups. My legs felt like rubber when we were done. Wendy put my bike in the trunk afterward and gave me a ride home. After that workout, we were both a little scared I wouldn't make it on my own.

Later, Mac and Em were over helping me rip my closet apart when I got a text from Connor. It said, "Meet us at the train. We'll give you a ride home after the game." We figured that "us" meant him and his parents.

Mac and Em acted like that was bad, but I was actually relieved. Parents always like me. It would make it easier. Plus, it meant that Connor wasn't embarrassed to be seen with me.

Anyway, they helped me pick out an outfit, and they told me how to fix my hair and makeup. But my stomach is in knots. And now I'm starting to worry again. Is this a date? Does he just feel sorry for me? Does he like me?

I need to stop freaking out and go to sleep.

Kat

Monday, July 9

"Us" ended up being Connor and his parents. They have season tickets, and his brother couldn't go today. Like I said, it was kind of a relief. After all, it was my first date. A one-on-one thing might have felt like too much pressure.

We sat away from them on the train because it was pretty full. We talked the whole time, of course. He asked if I had a boyfriend, and I'm sure I turned a thousand shades of red when I said I didn't.

The game was really fun. I've been to Met Stadium a thousand times, but this time was special.

His dad bought us hotdogs, but Connor and I both had veggie dogs with extra mustard.

His mom was super sweet. She talked to me about diets. She's not overweight at all, but she admitted that she's always worried about her weight. It was interesting to hear that from someone's mom. Aren't moms supposed to be past that stuff?

The game was awesome. We won. But to be honest, the best part was the ride back on the train. The car we were in was completely packed, so Connor and I were wedged in really close, and he held my hand the whole time. Not like a friend. Like a boyfriend. And he kept turning to look at me and smile.

Just now, I got a text from him. "I had a great time tonight. See you soon - C."

Kat

Tuesday, July 10

I went to the gym today, hoping I'd see Connor. I took longer than usual to lift my weights. I lingered on the treadmill, hoping he'd show up. But he didn't.

Later, I wanted to text him to see how he was doing, but I didn't. Mackenzie and Emily told me I couldn't. They said I'd look like a psycho.

But maybe I am a psycho. I don't feel normal right now. My stomach is in knots. I feel like every minute is consumed with thoughts of Connor and our date. I can't think about anything else.

I started to worry that I was actually going insane. I remember seeing a TV show once where the main character thinks she has a normal life, when in reality she's in a mental hospital and making all of it up. What if I imagined our whole date?

Then I decided it was crazier to be worrying about that than to be nervous the day after my first date. I kept myself busy by helping Mom make dinner (roasted chicken breasts, steamed broccoli and cauliflower, and brown rice).

I still wish he'd get in touch, though. If he doesn't like me, why did he hold my hand?

Kat

our meal: 292 calories
fried chicken, mashed potatoes,
gravy, and creamed corn: 622
calories

Wednesday, July 11

So the baseball game was two days ago, and I still haven't heard from Connor. I want to text him, but I don't want to seem pushy. Then again, I didn't text him back after he texted me on Monday night. What if he thinks I don't like HIM?

Okay. Update. I just texted him. All I said was, "Hey! Haven't see you at the gym this week. How's it going?"

Now I'm totally second-guessing myself. I shouldn't have texted him. I should have just waited. He's going to think I'm some kind of freak!

Update again. I just had lunch (whole wheat pita stuffed with leftover roasted chicken, steamed broccoli, and swiss cheese). I can't think of anything to do at home. It's been three hours since I texted Connor. No response. I'm going for a run. I'll still be going crazy, but at least I'll be getting some exercise and not sitting around in my room.

And I'm leaving my phone at home.

Kat

my lunch: 303 calories
grilled cheese and fries: 609

Thursday, July 12

Connor called! Finally! He had to go to his grandparents' for a couple of days to help them around the house, and he forgot his phone charger. So he didn't get my text until he got home. He said he realized he didn't know my last name, so he couldn't find me on Facebook. We friended each other as soon as we hung up. :)

So we talked for like half an hour. I tried to act normal, like it wasn't a big deal, but inside I was freaking out. Just for the first few minutes, though. After that, I felt really comfortable and calm talking to him. Like we've known each other a long time.

We talked about all sorts of stuff. He told me about his grandparents. They sound really sweet. I told him about how Grandpa died two years ago, and he was so nice about it. He asked me about memories I had of Grandpa and he really listened while I talked. Then we talked about school, Sarge, etc. It was so fun to talk to him.

Before he hung up, he asked if I'd go to a movie with him tomorrow. Obviously I said yes!

I called Mac right away. I think she was excited as I was. She's going to come over tomorrow to help me get ready. It is fabulous to have your own personal stylist!

Kat

Friday, July 13

I just woke up, and I realized that it is Friday the 13th. I'm kind of freaked out. That can't be good news for my date.

Update: I made sure I got my run done early, so I'd have time to take a long shower and get ready before my date. My date. I still can't believe it. A great, cute, smart, nice guy and I are going to the movies. Am I dreaming???

Update: I'm leaving for the mall in a few minutes. Mac and Em both came and helped me get ready. I think I look great. My clothes feel like they're not as tight. Good news for tomorrow's weigh-in?

Update: My heart is still pounding. Tonight was amazing. He was so sweet. He kissed my cheek when we met outside the movie theater, and he paid for my ticket. We went to the theater at the fancy mall, and they have the best snacks. We got an organic dried fruit and nut mix.

And we held hands the whole time.

When we were waiting for our rides home after the movie, he asked if I wanted to hang out again on Sunday night. Obviously I said yes. I told him I'd plan something amazing. Only problem is, now I actually have to think of something amazing!

So much for Friday the 13th. It was pretty much the best day ever.

Kat

bag of fruit and nuts: 490 calories
medium popcorn, soda, and junior
mints: 1278 calories

Saturday, July 14

I was so sure today was going to be great. Then I stepped on the scale, and I've only lost two more pounds.

My mom reminded me that two pounds is great, and that my body is building muscles at the same time that it loses fat.

I guess that's true. I mean, my clothes do fit better, and I can tell that I'm stronger. Still, I'd like to see more change in the number on the scale.

Eleven pounds total. Four pounds left. I know it's totally doable.

I hit the gym again today, because it was too hot to run outside. I can run two miles now without taking any breaks! It's so amazing to feel my body getting stronger.

After the gym, I hung out at Mac's for a while. She and Luke went on a couple of dates, but he quit his job at Scoop Shop and their relationship has kind of fizzled. She's not sad about it, so that's good. It's weird. Mac always has a boyfriend or at least someone she's crushing on. For the first time, I'm the one with the love life.

Kat

SUNDAY	MONDAY
15	**16**
* Sarge & Aunt Wendy 10 a.m. • • • • • • • • • • * Connor coming for dinner	William's baseball game

THURSDAY	FRIDAY
19	**20**
William's baseball game	Gym w/Connor

TUESDAY	WEDNESDAY
17 Party at Emily's Free day!!!	**18** Gym

SATURDAY	
21 Weigh-in	

Sunday, July 15

My meeting with Sarge was brutal this morning! I was dripping with sweat by the time she finally let Aunt Wendy and me go. But I'm set on losing the last bit of weight this week, so I made it through the whole workout.

Update: Connor came over tonight. We both love the Wizard of Oz, and it was on TV. So I invited him over to eat and watch the movie. Mom and Dad and William even made themselves scarce. They went over to the neighbors' for a while. I was so nervous. I like helping Mom cook, but I'd never made a whole meal all by myself.

I made veggie burgers in whole wheat pitas, sweet potato fries, steamed broccoli, and frozen yogurt with berries for dessert.

When Connor got to my house, I had just finished setting the table. I was wearing my favorite jeans and a cute red top. He looked adorable. I could tell he'd spent time on his hair.

We ate, and he loved all the food (or at least pretended to). Then we watched the movie. Mom and Dad came in halfway through and watched with us, which was fine. They weren't too embarrassing.

Then? Before he left? He kissed me.

Kat

my meal: 487 calories
hamburger, tater tots, peas,
ice cream sundae: 715 calories

Monday, July 16

I can't stop thinking about Connor. My first kiss. The way it feels to hold his hand. How it's kind of electric when we're sitting together and our shoulders touch. I went for a really long run this morning, but I barely even noticed how long it was because I was thinking about Connor the whole time.

I went over every minute of our date during my run and at William's baseball game. I still can't believe how well we get along. And I can't believe how I forget about everything when I'm with him.

I forget about all of the times I felt left out because my friends had boyfriends. I forget that there was ever a time when I felt bad about myself.

It's not that he does anything to make me feel that way. He's just being himself. But sometimes having another person around you that thinks you're okay just the way you are helps you believe it. And I never saw it coming. I never knew I was missing anything. I didn't know there was a way to feel better than I was feeling.

I'm not saying I only feel good because of him. Everything I'm doing this summer — eating better, getting over Josh, exercising, meeting Connor — is making me feel amazing. I feel like myself. Amazing.

Kat

Tuesday, July 17

Tonight we had another party at Emily's house. All of the usual people were there. I thought about bringing Connor, but I felt like it was a little early to throw him to the wolves. Mac and Em would question him for hours, asking about every detail of his life. I decided it wasn't time for that yet.

Here's the weirdest thing. Josh was there, and I think he was flirting with me! He told me that he had broken up with Alexis. They just didn't have anything in common. Then he started asking what I'd been doing with my summer, had I been to any baseball games lately, whatever.

So why was he doing that? Was it because some part of him realized that I wasn't into him anymore? Was it because I wasn't following him around like a puppy? Was it because I lost some weight?

I have no idea. He didn't leave my side all night. But even though a couple of weeks ago that's all I would have wanted, tonight it just irritated me. He doesn't make me feel like myself. I feel awkward and uncomfortable around him. Not at all how I feel around Connor.

Then I wished I would have invited him, and I was thrilled when I got a text from him just as I was leaving: "Thinking about you. Talk to you tomorrow."

Kat

Wednesday, July 18

As soon as I finished my morning run and had breakfast (yogurt, almonds, and berries), the first thing I did was check my email. Most of it was junk, but I had one message from Connor.

It was the best email I've ever gotten. He said he has a hard time saying things when we're together, so he wanted to write them down.

He likes me. He really likes me. He thinks I'm smart. He thinks I'm hysterical.

He thinks I'm beautiful.

I couldn't believe it when I read it.

I've never had a guy call me beautiful before. I mean, you know, besides Dad and Grandpa, obviously. But I have never had a boy tell me I was beautiful. I've never thought of myself as beautiful.

Wow.

I can't stop smiling.

I can't wait to see him again.

William has another game tomorrow. I invited Connor.

Kat

Thursday, July 19

As soon as I woke up I was sure I'd made a horrible mistake.

What was I thinking, inviting Connor? Watching a movie with my mom and dad was one thing. He didn't have to talk to them. Now he'll have to sit with them, and my dad will ask him a million questions. Is there any way I can get out of this???

Update: No. There is not. If I tried to cancel, it would hurt his feelings.

Update: What if Josh is there?

Update: Just got back from a run. This will be fine.

Update: I'm home. We picked him up, and everything was going just fine. Dad asked a few questions, found out he played football, and then they never ran out of things to talk about.

My other fear was seeing Josh, and we did. We ran into him between innings when we went to grab water at the concessions stand. I could tell he was surprised to see me with a guy. I'm not going to lie, it felt kind of great.

It was a fun day. But the best part was that when Connor introduced himself to Josh, he said, "Hey. I'm Kat's boyfriend, Connor."

Kat

Friday, July 20

I met Connor at the gym this morning. I thought it might be really awkward after last night, but it wasn't. Something about him relaxes me. I don't feel anxious or self-conscious. I feel calm.

My weigh-in is tomorrow. I'm a little nervous about it. I ate well all week, and I worked out as hard as I could without pushing myself TOO hard. I've been drinking tons of water, avoiding salty, fatty foods, and getting plenty of sleep.

Mom asked if I was going to stop exercising once I reach my goal.

I didn't even have to think about it. No way. I love
the way exercising makes me feel. And I love eating
healthy food. I feel so good inside, and I know it
shows on the outside, too.

Then Mom asked if I was still upset about not going
to fat camp. I had to think about that a while longer.
Obviously, I wouldn't have met Connor. But it would
have been nice to have people really telling me how
to do this. I've had to figure a lot of it out on my
own, and that's been hard. But then when I thought
about it, I realized that part was the best part. I know
I did this all by myself.

I just hope I meet my goal tomorrow. I really want to
go on vacation.

Kat

Saturday, July 21

So . . . I'm writing this from WildWater! Mom and Dad surprised me this morning by telling me that they'd already booked the vacation. They said they were so proud of me for all of the changes I've gone through this summer. And the best part was, I weighed in, and I was down five pounds. That's a total of SIXTEEN POUNDS.

I still have some weight to lose, but Connor said something interesting when I called to tell him about leaving on the trip. I filled him in on my whole weight-loss thing, and he said he'd never thought of me as overweight.

I was shocked. He said he thought of me as someone who was pretty, and smart, and funny. And he said that when he's around me, he feels like himself. Seriously, I almost cried.

I can't believe I did it. But I did. And I'm awesome. I can't believe I have a boyfriend. But I do. And he's fantastic.

And I've left out the best part. When I said we were going to WildWater, Connor started laughing. It turns out that his family is coming here for vacation too, on Wednesday! I can't wait to see him.

Kat

JULY

SUNDAY	MONDAY
22 *Vacation!!!*	**23**

THURSDAY	FRIDAY
26	**27**

TUESDAY	WEDNESDAY
24	**25** Connor arrives!!! Dinner w/Connor's family ♡

SATURDAY	
28 WildWater teen dance... ♡♡♡	★★★

Sunday, July 22

I love being on vacation. I spent all morning today lying on the beach, soaking up the sun and reading magazines. Then Mom and I walked down to the boardwalk for lunch. It's a couple of miles, so I figured it would be a great way to get a little exercise. It was the first time we've done anything athletic together in a long time. She was shocked by how much energy I had. I was wearing a comfortable skirt and a tank top, and she said she could really tell I was getting healthier.

It made me feel good to know she was noticing that kind of stuff. I'm old enough that I don't need my mom's approval on everything, but it's always nice to hear her say things like that.

We went to a little cafe for lunch. I think Mom thought we'd get burgers and fries and split a shake, but I didn't feel like eating all that salty stuff. I got a salad with grilled chicken, and Mom got soup and a sandwich. Afterward, she admitted that she was glad she hadn't overeaten.

Dad is grilling fish for dinner. I can't wait. And then we'll probably sit around playing cards. This is fun. But I still can't wait for Connor to get here!

Kat

Monday, July 23

Wednesday can't get here soon enough. I'm definitely having fun with my family, but there are so many fun things to do here that I want to do with Connor. There's a cool little movie theater, a park where musicians play all day, the beach . . .

WildWater has a lot of different places to stay. Most people stay in one of the hotels, because they have fancy water parks. My family always stays in a small cabin on the lake. I usually have to share a room with William, and my parents sleep on the sofa bed, but this year my parents upgraded to a two-bedroom, and William is sleeping on the couch.

I told him that's just the benefit of being the oldest. Anyway, Connor's family is staying in a cabin too. I hope it's near ours. It might be kind of cool to have our parents meet. On the other hand, that might be horrible.

I went swimming for a long time today with William. It was fun. I felt like a little kid again! We splashed each other and had races and then just floated for a long time, kind of talking and relaxing in our inner tubes. I wore a swimsuit! And I felt good about it!

Tonight I'm in charge of making dinner. We're having kebabs (my dad said he'd grill them for me). Chicken, shrimp, and tons of delicious vegetables. Yum!

Kat

Connor gets here tomorrow! It's almost midnight, so soon I'll be able to say Connor gets here TODAY! I can't wait.

My parents decided to invite him and his mom and dad over for dinner tomorrow night. I called him to ask about it, and he was so cute. He got really nervous and asked if they should bring anything and what they should wear and stuff. Adorable.

It turns out their cabin is just down the beach from us. Is it sickeningly romantic that I'm picturing long moonlit walks, barefoot through the waves . . . ??? Probably. But I am!

Mom and Dad sat me down tonight to talk about Connor. He's my first boyfriend, so obviously they're kind of freaked out about it. I made sure they knew that I was taking it slow. I did tell them that he kissed me, and I'm sure I turned bright red when I was talking about it. Embarrassing!

Anyway, they said they trusted me, and they said they liked Connor and were glad that he was such a nice guy. My dad made some dumb jokes about how he better not hurt me, blah blah blah. I just rolled my eyes, but I do think it's kind of sweet.

OMG. It's midnight! Connor IS COMING TODAY!!!!!!!!!!!

Kat

So, dinner with all of the parents was kind of awkward tonight. Mostly because I just wanted to be alone with Connor.

I think we both felt kind of nervous, and we wanted to be able to talk to each other without our parents around.

I think our parents liked each other, though. My mom made plans to go shopping with Connor's mom, and Connor's dad asked my dad if he wanted to go fishing with him. That's kind of cute.

I could tell poor William was completely bored the entire time, though.

After dinner, the parents all cleaned up. William
went to the resort arcade. So Connor and I were left
outside, sitting at the bonfire.

It was so peaceful and nice out. Warm, but not
hot. We just sat there, holding hands and talking,
for a really long time. I didn't realize how much
time had passed until my dad came out to get me.
He was wearing his pajamas—embarrassing! He
was like, "Okay, Kat, it's after midnight. Time to
say goodnight." Connor turned bright red and
apologized for keeping me out so late, but my dad
didn't seem mad at all.

When he and I walked inside, he told me he really
likes Connor. Then he added, "But mostly, I like how
happy you've seemed this summer."

Kat

Every summer, WildWater has these teen dances. Totally lame. But every time we've come here, I've secretly wanted to go. When I was little, it seemed so cool and glamorous. I'd see the older girls walking to the lodge where they have the dance. I'd hear the music playing late into the night. It always seemed like the absolute coolest thing to do.

Now I know it's probably not as cool as I always thought it was, but I still kind of want to go. Especially since now I have someone great to go with.

So my dilemma is, do I mention it to Connor?

Will he think I'm a huge loser if I want to go to the stupid dance? Probably. But I do want to go.

The dances are always on Saturdays. And I'm going home on Sunday morning. Connor will be here for another week and a half. It's so dumb, but I'm going to miss him!

We had a fun day today. In the morning, I hung out with my family. We had a nice long breakfast (egg white omelet with lots of veggies and salsa— yum!), and then went to the water park for a few hours. Then after lunch (leftover kabobs in a pita), Connor and I went swimming. I didn't even feel self-conscious in my swimsuit. We had a blast. I like him so much.

Kat

Friday, July 27

It occurred to me today that I can't weigh in tomorrow. It's so weird, I've gotten really used to my date with the scale on Saturday mornings. And for the first time, I don't think I'd be scared to step on it.

Not that I don't still need to lose weight. I do. Mom set up an appointment for me at the doctor when we get back, so I can find out what he thinks about my progress. She doesn't want me to lose weight too fast or do it in an unhealthy way. I don't think I'd want to either.

This has been hard enough! Plus, the whole point is being healthy . . .

Connor and his dad are fishing all day today, so
I won't see him until after dinner. I still haven't
mentioned the dance. I want to, but then again, I
don't want to.

I know he likes me. I guess I'm just worried that at
some point he'll find out that I'm really this big dork
and he won't like me anymore.

Kat

Saturday, July 28

This has been the best night of the best summer of my life. But let me start from the beginning.

I didn't see Connor all day today, and I was getting kind of worried about it. Maybe he'd finally realized that he was a gorgeous, smart, funny guy who should have a gorgeous, smart, funny girlfriend.

After dinner, my mom told me to put on a dress and some makeup and she'd take me out. I'd brought one dress in case we went out for a fancy dinner or something. I thought she was just trying to cheer me up. I was feeling pretty down.

I didn't feel like sitting around, so I got ready. Mom and I walked up toward the lodge. I could hear the sounds of the dance getting started. That's when I started feeling really depressed. It was such a dumb thing to feel bad about, but I felt like Connor was done with me.

Then I saw him. Wearing a suit and holding a bouquet of wildflowers. Mom squeezed my arm and headed back to the cabin. Connor gave me the flowers and said, "I picked these for you."

When he walked me back to my cabin after the dance, he said, "This has been the best summer of my life." And for so many reasons, I said, "Mine too."

Kat

You can lose it too!

(just make sure you talk
to your doctor first)

turkey burgers

- 1 lb ground turkey breast
- 2 tablespoons finely chopped onion
- 1 jalapeño, seeds and ribs removed, chopped
- pepper, cumin, and coriander (or whatever spices you like best!)
- 1 egg
- 1/4 cup whole wheat breadcrumbs

Combine!

Form into patties.

Spray a pan with cooking spray. Cook over medium high heat until burgers are cooked through.

Trying to cut carbs? Try chopping romaine lettuce, onion, tomato, and green pepper. Cut up a turkey burger, and top it all with salsa.

In a blender, combine:

- 1/2 cup lowfat yogurt
- 1 big handful of washed spinach
- 1 banana
- 1/2 cup blueberries (frozen or fresh)
- 1/4 cup lowfat milk

Blend and enjoy!

You can also add other fresh or frozen fruit, and try different flavors of yogurt to give yourself a new taste experience.
If you're trying to add protein to your diet, try including silken tofu or protein powder.

healthy breakfast ideas

*egg-white omelet with your favorite veggies

*whole-grain toast with peanut butter, milk

*grapefruit, cottage cheese, and tea

*homemade granola with yogurt

*steel-cut oats with dried berries and milk

*a smoothie — make sure it has protein to help get you through the morning

*scrambled egg whites, avocado, and tomatoes in a whole-wheat tortilla

*fresh fruit and yogurt

(**What not to eat**: Don't overload your system with tons of sugar or fat. Ease in to the morning!)

*lots of crisp, fresh veggies: dip into hummus for some extra protein, or make your own dip out of low-fat sour cream and your favorite spices

*grapes! delicious when frozen

*a sliced apple and peanut butter

*gazpacho: chop lots of veggies, add tomato juice, blend, and keep in the fridge

*a handful of almonds

*air-popped popcorn

Don't forget: junk food isn't off limits. Just limit the portion size!

- green pepper
- zucchini
- yellow squash
- cherry tomatoes
- mushrooms
- red onion
- chicken breast, skin and bone removed

Chop everything except tomatoes into 1-inch pieces. Put everything in a large bowl. Toss with a little olive oil, salt, and pepper.

Thread onto skewers. (If you're using wooden skewers, soak them first.)

Grill until chicken is cooked through.

Not crazy about something on the list? Use your favorite veggies!

You're more than a number.
Every day, whether or not you're trying to lose weight,
take time to appreciate yourself. Here's an easy way:

Make a you're great cheat sheet!

* Write down 5 things you like about yourself.

* Write down 5 things other people like about you.

* Write down 5 things you're good at.

* Write down 5 things you'd like to learn.

* Write down the names of 5 people you love.

* Write down 5 favorite memories.

* Write down 5 things you're looking forward to.

* Write down 5 places you love to go.

* Write down 5 places you've never been to, but you'd love to visit.

* Write down 5 things that make you happy.

If you're feeling down, just look at your cheat sheet.

Calorie counting can be tricky. Every person needs a different number of calories every day. And two people who weigh the same amount may need different numbers; your caloric need is based on your metabolism, which is affected by your size and your activity level.

If you're trying to lose weight, make sure you're still taking in enough calories. Weight loss is as much about exercising and eating whole, nutritious foods as it is about cutting calories.

Try keeping track of your food in a food journal. Recording what you eat often helps ensure that you make good choices.

If you need help determining what, how much, and how often to eat, please seek the advice of a qualified nutritionist. Your doctor is the best person to ask for recommendations in your area.

Experts recommend that teenagers get **60 minutes of exercise** every day. But that doesn't mean you have to kill yourself on the treadmill for an hour. Just keep active. Chase your little brother around; take a walk with your mom; play fetch with the family dog. Studies have shown that teenagers who stayed active were less likely to be significantly overweight than teenagers who spent more time being sedentary.

Weight loss =
stay active
+ eat right
+ don't eat too much

Don't cut back on social time to include exercise. Go swimming, spend time biking, join a yoga class, or find a fun DVD that you AND your friends can enjoy.

Natalie Kath was born and raised in Minnesota. Growing up, Natalie always struggled with her weight. In 2010, she made the decision to lose weight and get healthy for good. Natalie enjoys playing with her nieces and nephew, knitting, listening to music, attempting to golf, spending time with friends, reading, watching and playing sports, and working out. She currently writes a blog about her weight-loss experience and her continuing effort to live a healthy lifestyle.